Tim Hardaway

Additional Titles in the Sports Reports *Series*

Andre Agassi
Star Tennis Player
(0-89490-798-0)

Troy Aikman
Star Quarterback
(0-89490-927-4)

Roberto Alomar
Star Second Baseman
(0-7660-1079-1)

Charles Barkley
Star Forward
(0-89490-655-0)

Terrell Davis
Star Running Back
(0-7660-1331-6)

Tim Duncan
Star Forward
(0-7660-1334-0)

Dale Earnhardt
Star Race Car Driver
(0-7660-1335-9)

Brett Favre
Star Quarter Back
(0-7660-1332-4)

Jeff Gordon
Star Race Car Driver
(0-7660-1083-X)

Wayne Gretzky
Star Center
(0-89490-930-4)

Ken Griffey, Jr.
Star Outfielder
(0-89490-802-2)

Scott Hamilton
Star Figure Skater
(0-7660-1236-0)

Anfernee Hardaway
Star Guard
(0-7660-1234-4)

Grant Hill
Star Forward
(0-7660-1078-3)

Allen Iverson
Star Guard
(0-7660-1501-7)

Michael Jordan
Star Guard
(0-89490-482-5)

Shawn Kemp
Star Forward
(0-89490-929-0)

Jason Kidd
Star Guard
(0-7660-1333-2)

Michelle Kwan
Star Figure Skater
(0-7660-1504-1)

Tara Lipinski
Star Figure Skater
(0-7660-1505-X)

Dan Marino
Star Quarterback
(0-89490-933-9)

Mark Messier
Star Center
(0-89490-801-4)

Reggie Miller
Star Guard
(0-7660-1082-1)

Randy Moss
Star Wide Receiver
(0-7660-1503-3)

Chris Mullin
Star Forward
(0-89490-486-8)

Hakeem Olajuwon
Star Center
(0-89490-803-0)

Shaquille O'Neal
Star Center
(0-89490-656-9)

Gary Payton
Star Guard
(0-7660-1330-8)

Scottie Pippen
Star Forward
(0-7660-1080-5)

Jerry Rice
Star Wide Receiver
(0-89490-928-2)

Cal Ripken, Jr.
Star Shortstop
(0-89490-485-X)

David Robinson
Star Center
(0-89490-483-3)

Barry Sanders
Star Running Back
(0-89490-484-1)

Deion Sanders
Star Athlete
(0-89490-652-6)

Junior Seau
Star Linebacker
(0-89490-800-6)

Emmitt Smith
Star Running Back
(0-89490-653-4)

Frank Thomas
Star First Baseman
(0-89490-659-3)

Thurman Thomas
Star Running Back
(0-89490-445-0)

Chris Webber
Star Forward
(0-89490-799-9)

Tiger Woods
Star Golfer
(0-7660-1081-3)

Steve Young
Star Quarterback
(0-89490-654-2)

SPORTS REPORTS

Tim Hardaway
Star Guard

Bert Rosenthal

Enslow Publishers, Inc.
40 Industrial Road   PO Box 38
Box 398   Aldershot
Berkeley Heights, NJ 07922   Hants GU12 6BP
USA   UK
http://www.enslow.com

Copyright © 2001 by Bert Rosenthal

All rights reserved.

No part of this book may be reproduced by any means without the written permission of the publisher.

Library of Congress Cataloging-in-Publication Data

Rosenthal, Bert.
   Tim Hardaway : star guard / Bert Rosenthal.
      p. cm. — (Sports reports)
   Includes bibliographical references (p.) and index.
   ISBN 0-7660-1500-9
   1. Hardaway, Tim, 1966—Juvenile literature. 2. Basketball players—United States—Biography—Juvenile literature. [1. Hardaway, Tim, 1966– . 2. Basketball players. 3. Afro-Americans—Biography.] I. Title. II. Series
   GV884.H243 R68 2001

796.323′092—dc21

   00-009955

Printed in the United States of America

10 9 8 7 6 5 4 3 2 1

To Our Readers:
All Internet Addresses were active and appropriate when we went to press. Any comments or suggestions can be sent by e-mail to Comments@enslow.com or to the address on the back cover.

Photo Credits: © NBA Entertainment. Photo by Andy Hayt, p. 63; © NBA Entertainment. Photo by Barry Gossage, p. 26; © NBA Entertainment. Photo by Fernando Medina, pp. 24, 36; © NBA Entertainment. Photo by Jon Hayt, pp. 11, 15, 79, 81, 86; © NBA Entertainment. Photo by Layne Murdoch, p. 84; © NBA Entertainment. Photo by Nathaniel S. Butler, pp. 58, 71, 88; © NBA Entertainment. Photo by Noren Trotman, p. 74; © NBA Entertainment. Photo by Sam Forencich, pp. 48, 55, 67; © NBA Entertainment. Photo by Tim Defrisco, p. 40;

Cover Photo: © NBA Entertainment. Photo by Jon Hayt

Contents

1 The Game 7

2 Growing Up in Chicago 19

3 High School and College 29

4 Turning Pro 39

5 Golden, Then Not So Golden 51

6 Heating Up in Miami 61

7 Tim Hardaway Is In Charge 77

Chapter Notes 94

Career Statistics 99

Where to Write
and Internet Addresses 101

Index 102

Chapter 1

The Game

In the relatively short time that the Miami Heat had been in the National Basketball Association (NBA), the team had developed a bitter rivalry with the New York Knicks. The Knicks had been in the league for quite some time, so they had a long time to develop heated competition against other teams. For now, though, their focus was on the Heat.

Perhaps the Knicks felt that Miami's coach, Pat Riley, had abandoned the Knicks when he left for the warmer climate of Florida after the 1994–95 season. Riley had coached the Knicks for four seasons, starting in 1991–92. During those years, the Knicks compiled some of the best records in the team's history—51–31, 60–22, 57–25, and 55–27.

Under Riley, the Knicks won three Atlantic Division titles and finished second once. The team also narrowly missed winning the NBA Championship in 1994, losing to the Houston Rockets in a dramatic seventh game of the Finals.

Under Coach Riley, the Knicks had established themselves as one of the league's premier teams. They felt they were destined eventually to win a league championship. Since Riley's departure, the Knicks' record had slipped. Meanwhile, Riley had turned the Heat into one of the NBA's most respected teams.

When the two teams met in the playoffs for the first time, the atmosphere was intense. The occasion was the Eastern Conference Semifinals, a best-of-seven series that began on May 7, 1997, during Pat Riley's second season as Miami's coach.

One year later, when the teams met again in the playoffs, Miami forward P. J. Brown expressed these feelings toward the Knicks:

> You've got to be scared of a team that knows your every play. We don't play our best against them for some reason, and they play their best against us for some reason. They're a totally different team against us than they are against anybody else. They play harder. The intensity is at a whole other level.

FACT

The Miami Heat were formally granted an NBA franchise on April 22, 1987. Expansion franchises also were granted to Orlando, Charlotte, and Minnesota. Miami and Charlotte began playing during the 1988–89 season. Orlando and Minnesota started the following season.

> They have an aura. An aura that comes when they put on that jersey. . . . Kind of like putting on a Superman suit. How's that?[1]

Tim Hardaway, Miami's star guard, was not awed by the Knicks at that first playoff meeting. Especially not by Chris Childs, who was going to be matched up against him. Hardaway was still angry about some comments that Childs had made about him earlier in the season.

Hardaway said of Childs:

> He got up there [to New York] and all of a sudden started talking a lot. He talked a lot of stuff the first game we played them when we beat them up there. He was saying I can take him. All I know is in New Jersey [where Childs played previously], he was a nice, quiet guy. Now with the Knicks, he's trying to be tough and this and that.
>
> I guess that's what you've got to do when you're with the Knicks; you've got to be tough. . . . I don't understand it. So that's why every time we play I put him in his place. A lot of people don't understand that I can go out there and talk a lot of stuff and get another player out of their game, but still play my game.[2]

Hardaway also talked about the Heat's attitude toward the Knicks. He said,

We're two teams that don't like each other. It's as simple as that. I'm from the old school. I have a lot of respect for the Knicks, but once you're in between the white lines, the [heck] with 'em. That's the way I am.[3]

During the 1996–97 season, the Knicks won the series between the teams, 3–1. They also got the jump in the opening playoff game, winning 88–79 at Miami, with the help of a 16–0 scoring run in the third quarter. Game 2 was another defensive struggle. This time the Heat won, 88–84, as Hardaway scored a playoff career high and set a Miami postseason record with 34 points. He also had 8 rebounds and 4 assists. Hardaway's running one-hander in the final minute of the game gave Miami the lead for good, 85–84. Twenty-five of Hardaway's points came in the first half, when the Heat rallied from an early 10-point deficit.

The series moved to New York for Game 3, and the Knicks regained the lead, winning a low-scoring contest, 77–73. With the score at 76–73, and with less than three seconds remaining, Hardaway tried to hit a game-tying three-pointer. Seven-foot Patrick Ewing, a foot taller than Hardaway, blocked it.

New York then moved to the brink of clinching the series by winning Game 4 at home, 89–76. That made four consecutive games in which neither team

Tim Hardaway goes up for a shot with a defender looking on.

had scored 90 or more points. Actually, that should not have been too surprising. While both teams had compiled impressive winning records during the regular season—Miami was 61–21, New York was 57–25—both relied more on defense than on offense.

Game 5 turned out to be the key game of the series, not so much for the result, but because of what happened with less than two minutes left. The Heat were fighting for survival. They broke open a close game with a 17–2 scoring run during the fourth quarter and went on to win, 96–81. But with 1:53 remaining in the game, New York's frustrations boiled over. The Knicks' Charlie Ward undercut P. J. Brown during a successful Hardaway free throw. Brown fought back by throwing Ward to the floor.

Four Knicks—Patrick Ewing, Allan Houston, John Starks, and Larry Johnson—came off the bench to join the fight. When the officials and security people finally got everyone untangled, Ward, Starks, and Brown were ejected from the game.

More important, the league ruled after the game that Ward, Ewing, and Houston would be suspended for Game 6 as punishment for their part in the brawl. Starks and Johnson would be suspended for Game 7, if there should be a seventh game. Brown was suspended for both games, but his loss was not as damaging to the Heat as were the absences of the

FACT

The Miami Heat made their first playoff appearance on April 24, 1992, losing to the Chicago Bulls, 113–92, in an opening-round game. The Heat lost the series, three games to none, and did not get their first playoff victory until two years later, when they beat the Atlanta Hawks, 93–88.

Knicks' players to New York. Ewing, Starks, Houston, and Johnson were the Knicks' four top scorers, and Ward was one of their best playmakers. Brown, on the other hand, was more of a defensive force than an offensive threat.

With Ewing and Houston missing from Game 6, New York was forced to use two of its reserves—Buck Williams and John Starks—as starters. With Ward also gone, the bench was short on reserves. Still, New York hung tough. The undermanned Knicks led, 66–64, going into the final period, before wilting. With Alonzo Mourning taking advantage of Ewing's absence to score 28 points, Miami rallied to win, 95–90.

Miami had tied the series at three games each and would have home-court advantage for Game 7. Miami's spirits were high, while New York was reeling. Again the Knicks were shorthanded, with Starks and Johnson out.

Led by Tim Hardaway, who was hitting shots from all over the floor, the Heat opened leads of 25–14 after one quarter and 49–32 by halftime. In the first period, the Heat fell behind, 6–2, then reeled off eighteen straight points. A sellout crowd of 14,870 was perhaps the loudest, most enthusiastic in Miami basketball history. The fans cheered and yelled continuously. The Heat still led by seventeen points after three periods. The score was 71–54. Hardaway made five consecutive shots, the final three from three-point range. During the period, he scored 18 of Miami's 22 points. He could not remember ever having played that well in a single quarter.

Despite a mild Knicks rally in the fourth quarter, Miami won the game, 101–90, and the series, 4–3. Miami had become only the sixth team in playoff history to overcome a 3–1 deficit to win a series. Hardaway again exceeded his single-game postseason high and set another franchise record with 38 points. He also had game highs in assists (7) and steals (5) and connected on 6-of-10 three-point shots.

"I was tuning the fans out," Hardaway said of the noisy crowd, "because I was doing my thing. When I'm in that zone, you're at my mercy."[4] "Hardaway shot the ball like he was on the playground," the Knicks' Buck Williams said. "We said all along that he's the head of this basketball team."[5]

Allan Houston could not believe the Knicks had lost the series after leading, 3–1. "There's no way to describe it," he said. "It's disbelief. It's a shock."[6] It was not a shock to the Heat. They had seen Hardaway perform such heroics many times. In fact, he had done it in the Heat's first-round playoff series that year, hitting a clutch three-pointer, with

Tim Hardaway shows his emotions on the court. In the many series the Heat have played against the Knicks, Hardaway has had plenty of opportunities for emotional responses.

14.1 seconds left and another late basket, to seal Miami's fifth-game victory over the Orlando Magic.

"He's virtually unstoppable," Miami's Dan Majerle said of Hardaway. "We've seen it so many times, but never in a game like this."[7]

The Knicks' Charles Oakley also was impressed with Hardaway's clutch performance. "Just when it looked like we were going to make a run, he broke our backs," Oakley said.[8] Hardaway was satisfied with his performance. He had engineered a remarkable comeback victory for the Heat. He had done it against Miami's most hated rival, the Knicks. And he had done it to his early-season tormentor, Chris Childs. While Hardaway shot a magnificent 12-of-20 from the field and 8-of-10 from the foul line, Childs was only 2-for-9 from the field and 1-for-2 from the foul line, for 6 points. Childs got so frustrated that he kicked the ball into the stands midway through the fourth quarter.

Hardaway also helped torture the Knicks' backcourt into committing 11 fouls—six by Ward, five by Childs. Ward, who had ignited the brawl in Game 5, was booed every time he touched the ball before fouling out with 1:06 remaining. The fouls were a big part of the game. While New York outscored Miami from the field, 37–30, the Heat won the game at the foul line. They converted 30-of-42 to only 10-of-13 for the Knicks.

Hardaway was not the only pleased member of the Miami organization. All of the players and the entire coaching staff were thrilled at having beaten the Knicks, especially after Patrick Ewing had boldly predicted a New York victory. "We won the Atlantic Division and they [the Knicks] were saying it was no big deal," Majerle said. "It feels good to get rid of them."[9]

"It wasn't a thing that we won the series because they didn't have their players," Miami's Ike Austin said. "They cracked under pressure. We made them pay for it."[10]

A sign in the Miami Arena after the game read "P.J. M.V.P."[11] This meant that P. J. Brown should have been named Most Valuable Player after helping get a total of five Knicks sidelined for the final two games. While Brown's accomplishment was a big plus for the Heat, Miami could not have won the series without the heroics of Tim Hardaway.

As the final seconds of Game 7 ticked down, Hardaway let out a shout and scanned the stands until his eyes met those of his wife and his father. "We're going to Chicago," Hardaway shouted. "We're on our way home."[12]

Chapter 2
Growing Up in Chicago

Tim Hardaway was speaking literally when he said he was going home to Chicago after the Heat beat the Knicks in the second round of the playoffs. Hardaway was born in Chicago, Illinois, on September 1, 1966.

Miami's next opponent in the playoffs was the Chicago Bulls. The Heat had lost three straight games to the Bulls in the opening round of the playoffs in 1996. Now the Heat and Hardaway were hoping to get revenge against Michael Jordan and the Bulls—starting in Hardaway's hometown. Jordan, a native of North Carolina, had become the pride of Chicago, after leading the Bulls to four NBA titles. He would win two more championships before retiring after the 1997–98 season.

Miami's players were still seeking their first NBA Championship. If they were successful, Hardaway would regain some of the fan base he had lost to the popular Michael Jordan in Chicago. As it turned out, the Bulls again spoiled Hardaway's homecoming. They won the Eastern Conference Finals, four games to one. Hardaway was not much of a factor in the first three games. He scored a total of only 34 points on 11-of-39 shooting from the field.

When he finally broke loose in Game 4, scoring 25 points and contributing a game-high 7 assists, the Heat won, 87–80. He also was outstanding in Game 5, registering 27 points and 5 assists. Those numbers were not enough, however. Chicago won, 100–87, to end the series.

For the second straight year, Hardaway had been beaten by his hometown Bulls and Michael Jordan. He had, however, gained the respect of the Chicago players and coaching staff for his toughness, particularly in the final two games. Tim Hardaway was a fierce competitor who grew up on the playgrounds of Chicago's South Side. He played at the same high school as had NBA All-Stars Cazzie Russell and Terry Cummings.

Before he got to Carver High School, though, he survived some difficult times. When Tim was eleven years old, his parents divorced. It saddened him deeply. "I can't forgive that,"' Hardaway said later. "They used to fight all the time. . . . I thought, 'We are a family, and you are letting us down.'"[1] All he wanted was for his parents to love each other. It did not work out that way, however. After his parents' divorce, Tim went to live with his maternal grandmother, Minnie E. Eubanks.

"My mom and dad got divorced when I was in the fifth grade, and my grandmother was there to help me cope with it," Hardaway said.

> I took it real hard. It was like, "Man, why are you getting divorced? You all are supposed to be married forever." It was something I'd never experienced and something I don't want to experience in my marriage, because it was ugly and painful to me. But my grandmother, she helped me and my brother endure it. We stayed with her. She said to just go on with our lives. She helped me get my mind off it and get my mind back into school.[2]

Tim Hardaway has never forgotten the lessons his grandmother taught him. She helped him survive after the breakup of his parents' marriage. She helped him get passing grades in school (except when he was in the eighth grade, which he had to repeat). She taught him much about life. She encouraged him to pursue his dreams. She taught him to read from the Bible. She preached the lessons of the late Dr. Martin Luther King, Jr. She also insisted Tim take care of his mother.

Hardaway's grandmother died in the summer of 1990. He keeps her memory alive by wearing the letters MEE on the backs of his sneakers. Speaking of his grandmother, Hardaway said, "She taught me to roll with the punches. She told me to be a leader. Don't be a follower. Always be somebody."[3]

Tim's father, Donald Hardaway, also played an important part in his son's basketball career. When Tim was six months old, his mother, a mail carrier, put a toy car in his crib. His father, who was a well-known basketball player and a truck driver in Chicago, put a basketball in the crib. Tim threw out the car and lay down with the ball. He and a basketball have been virtually inseparable ever since.

Basketball became Tim's release. He loved the game when he was a little boy. Then, when his parents were having marital problems, basketball became something more. The basketball court was a place to get away. It was his refuge. "When I was going through stuff . . . I could get my frustrations worked out just by playing hard—drills, shooting, playing against people," Hardaway said. "Just taking it out. . . ."[4]

Another place Tim went was to the house of Donald Pitman, his coach at Kohn Elementary

School. Hardaway spent many nights at Pitman's house rather at his own home. Pitman consoled Tim, the point guard who was not yet five feet tall.

Coach Pitman wanted to make certain that Tim would not get hurt any more. So he brought him home. When Tim went back to his own house, he often would cry himself to sleep. Tim's mother tried to be a stabilizing influence on her sons. She wanted a comforting home for them.

Tim's father and mother taught him not to be a quitter, not to give up, so Tim was not afraid to fight back. He has carried his parents' teachings into adulthood, but he does not fight with his hands or fists. He retaliates on the basketball court by trying harder, or by trying to outplay his opponent. Most times he has succeeded. When he succeeds, he is gratified and has a great feeling of accomplishment.

In fact, because of what he has accomplished, Hardaway is considered an overachiever. By professional basketball standards, he is not a big man. He is six feet tall, but appears smaller. Even at that height, most players in the NBA tower over him. The same situation existed when he was younger. He just was not as big as the other kids. He never backed down from a challenge, though. "I have dealt with adversity from Day 1," Hardaway said. "In grammar school, high school, and college, I was

FACT

When Tim Hardaway is not playing basketball, he does many other things. He also enjoys spending time with his family, watching movies, and listening to music. Two of his favorite musical artists are R. Kelly and Janet Jackson.

By professional basketball standards, Tim Hardaway is not a big player. At just six feet tall, most players in the NBA tower over him.

too short. A lot of people counted me out real quick."⁵ That was a mistake on their part.

Hardaway proved to everyone that he could play well despite his lack of size. He also showed he could overcome his problems at home. "He was always controlled," Donald Pitman said. "Tim is not a fighter. He would take it out on you on the court. He could embarrass a guy. The anger and frustration he felt, he vented it on the basketball court."⁶

As Tim grew older, he gathered strength from his grandmother, his mother, his coaches, and his teachers. He also developed his game. He carried his basketball everywhere and played both before and after school. People in the neighborhood would joke that Tim used to wake up everyone within earshot by dribbling his ball to the bus stop. He was so into the game that he told anyone who would listen that someday he was going to play in the NBA. At the time, it seemed like a joke. People laughed; he was too small. That tag always haunted him. When confronted with it, Tim played harder. He would not let anything stop him. He was driven to show that he could play with the best.⁷

Sure, he had to overcome tough times, but he would not be intimidated. He was told he would not be able to play defense, that he would not be able to cover bigger players. But he was always quick

FACT

Tim Hardaway donates ten dollars for each assist he has in a game to the American Cancer Society, as a tribute to Bob Walters. Walters, his high school coach, died of cancer in 1987.

Tim Hardaway does not like to take no for an answer when he is told he cannot accomplish something on the court.

enough, always strong enough. He would not back down. He raced up and down the court, playing solid defense as well as offense. He proved he could compete.

Basketball was going to be his ticket to the world of professional sports.

Chapter 3
High School and College

Tim Hardaway matured quickly. By the sixth grade, he was running the offense for the eighth-grade basketball team at Kohn Middle School—a rare honor. At Carver High School, Hardaway started at point guard as a freshman, an even rarer occurrence. In his senior year, in 1985, he took Carver to the final game of the Chicago city championship for the first time since the 1960s. It was not a successful trip, however. The team lost to San Simeon.

Unlike his father, Tim completed high school. Donald Hardaway had dropped out after his sophomore year and enlisted in the U.S. Army. Tim wanted to go on with his education. He was planning a career in criminal justice. With his basketball skills, he hoped to get an athletic scholarship to a college or a university. College and university scouts had often watched him play, but Hardaway did not get many offers.

When an offer did come from the University of Texas-El Paso (UTEP), Hardaway grabbed it. He would now get an opportunity to play basketball and pursue his education. Basketball was important to him, and UTEP had a highly respected basketball program. Its coach, Don "The Bear" Haskins, was one of the best-known coaches in the country. Haskins was impressed immediately with Hardaway's ability to palm a basketball. (A player who palms a basketball holds onto the top of the ball with one palm, facing down.) The big players did it easily, but few players of Hardaway's size have big enough hands. "He's extra, extra strong," Haskins said. "Look at his hands—he's five-foot eleven inches [tall] and can hold a basketball in one hand."[1]

As a freshman at UTEP, Hardaway did not play much. In twenty-eight games, he started only three, and averaged about fifteen minutes and 4.1 points per game. Those numbers increased considerably during his sophomore year. He started thirty of thirty-one games, and averaged nearly thirty minutes and 10 points. In his junior year, he played in thirty-two games, averaging more than thirty-two minutes and 13.6 points. While his scoring totals were not those of a superstar, Hardaway had become an efficient player. He was the Miners' leader. That efficiency was proven by his 183 assists, a school record, during his junior year. He had helped direct the team to a 75–22 record over three seasons. He had led UTEP to two Western Athletic Conference (WAC) championships and three straight NCAA tournament appearances. He was chosen for the All-Conference Second Team as a junior. He might have made the first team if not for an ankle injury that slowed him for five games. He led the WAC in assists (5.7 per game) and steals (2.4 per game). He had perhaps his best game of the season in the first round of the NCAA tournament. In a loss to Wyoming, he had 21 points, 9 assists, 6 rebounds, and 5 steals.

Hardaway's senior season turned out to be his best overall. He started all thirty-three of UTEP's games, and averaged 36 minutes, 22 points, 5.4 assists, and 4 rebounds. Of all the figures, the rebounding total was most remarkable. For a player who often was the smallest on the floor, averaging 4 rebounds per game made him seem like a giant.

Tim Hardaway finished his college career with 1,586 points in 124 games, making him UTEP's

FACT

Tim Hardaway is always eager to help people who are unable to help themselves. He once flew forty children with cancer to Sea World in Florida.

all-time scoring leader. He also averaged 4.5 assists and 2.1 steals per game. He was chosen the conference's Player of the Year as a senior. He was also selected the Most Valuable Player at one postseason All-Star Game and MVP in another postseason exhibition tournament. Because he was listed in UTEP's basketball guide at five feet eleven inches instead of six feet as he is in the NBA guide, he was awarded the Frances Pomeroy Naismith Memorial Basketball Hall of Fame Award as the nation's outstanding senior college player under six feet tall.

"I've been fortunate in my years at UTEP by having a number of outstanding players," Coach Haskins said. "I cannot recall having anyone better than Tim Hardaway."[2]

Hardaway was a popular player in college. As a child, he had received the nickname Tim Bug, because people said he scooted around the basketball court like a little bug. He also had developed a funny kind of shot. It would float toward the basket with little spin, or sometimes none at all, almost like a knuckleball baseball pitch. "Many people have tried to change it," Hardaway said during his sophomore year at UTEP. "But I know that if I try something different, I'm not going to feel comfortable. My high school coach just told me to shoot like you want to make it every time. I know that my percentage isn't that good, but Coach Haskins wants me to work harder on improving it."[3]

Hardaway's ability to think quickly also was a big factor in his improving play. He said,

> When you go in for a layup, you can't always think about making it. Sometimes you've got to think about passing it out or drawing a foul from the big guy inside.[4]

Just about everyone who watched Hardaway recognized and appreciated his skills. Antonio Davis, UTEP's starting center and later a member of the Toronto Raptors, was among the admirers. "Tim's a great player," Davis said. "You just can't stop him because he can do so much. I'm glad I'm playing with him instead of against him. He's been playing a long time and practicing for so long."[5]

Another person who was impressed by Hardaway's play was Utah's coach, Lynn Archibald. "He's really a strong guard," Archibald said. "I think he's one of the best guards on the West Coast, if not the best. He has great acceleration to the basket, and I think his strength accounts for that."[6] Hardaway's own coach, Don Haskins, said he never doubted Hardaway would make it big as a pro. Haskins realized that Hardaway was terrific in the open court, he was an excellent passer, he had outstanding court vision, and he worked hard in the gym to perfect his skills. Haskins compared Hardaway to a former UTEP player, Nate "Tiny" Archibald.

Archibald was another small guard, standing only six feet one inch tall. He attended the University of Texas-El Paso from 1967 to 1970. Archibald went on to become one of the greatest players in NBA history. He was elected to the Naismith Memorial Basketball Hall of Fame in 1990 and to the NBA's Fiftieth Anniversary All-Time Team in 1996. In thirteen seasons in the league, he averaged 18.8 points per game and played in five All-Star games. He was named the All-Star Game's MVP in 1981. He is the only player to lead the NBA in scoring and assists in the same season, averaging 34.0 points and 11.4 assists in the 1972–73 season. Archibald was selected to the All-NBA first team three times and the second team twice. He also played with the 1980–81 league champions, the Boston Celtics.

With all of Archibald's talent, it was gratifying to Hardaway to know that his coach compared the two of them so favorably. Just like Archibald, Hardaway made everyone forget about his height. His strength, speed, and aggressiveness more than made up for that deficiency.

> **FACT**
>
> One of Tim Hardaway's favorite holiday memories was getting a dog for Christmas. When he was about seven or eight years old, he really wanted a dog. He got his wish and named the dog Cuddles. He loved the dog and took care of him, walking him every day.

"I'm not intimidated by anybody," said Hardaway. "I go out there and fight, kick, claw, bite—do whatever it takes."[7] Hardaway did not mean that literally. He does not fight, kick, claw, or bite anyone. He just meant that he plays very hard, as hard as he can, to win. The basketball court is a safe place for him. That is where he takes out his mental frustrations. He talks tough and sometimes appears tough, but he never loses his cool on the court. That ability to keep his cool is the sign of a mature and knowledgeable player. Hardaway is both. He is able to keep his emotions under control without getting physically violent. He remains levelheaded at all times.

"You're going to take some bruises, but get right up," Hardaway's father told him when he was young. "Show 'em you're not a punk or a crybaby. Show 'em you can take a hit."[8]

"It [basketball] was always my release," Hardaway said. "When I was going through stuff with my dad, I could get my frustrations worked out just by playing hard—drills, shooting, playing against people."[9]

During Hardaway's freshman year at UTEP, his father apologized for all the pain he had caused his family. He deeply regretted what he had done. Much of his newfound affection was directed

The basketball court is a "safe haven" for Tim Hardaway. He can take out his mental frustrations by playing the best game he can.

toward his son. "Tim means everything to me," Donald Hardaway said. "He was my first-born male child and I love him. I want him to know that."[10]

While Tim Hardaway may have a hard edge on the court, he is very pleasant away from the basketball floor and in the locker room. He smiles and laughs often. His smile makes people feel like he has known them for a long time. His loud laugh often echoes throughout the locker room.

After his highly successful college career, Hardaway was ready for the pros. In the 1989 pre-draft camps, he played very well. It appeared that he would be a very high pick. However, perhaps because of his size, teams may have been afraid to take a chance on such a relatively small player. They wanted size, and Hardaway did not measure up. On draft day, he was chosen as the fourteenth pick in the first round by the Golden State Warriors. Still, Tim Hardaway had to take some consolation in that number. His star predecessor at UTEP, Nate Archibald, was picked nineteenth in the 1970 draft, by the Cincinnati Royals.

Now Tim Hardaway had to get ready to start his NBA career with a team that had reached the second round of the playoffs the previous season. It boasted such stars as Chris Mullin and Mitch Richmond. Could Hardaway meet the challenge?

Chapter 4

Turning Pro

When Tim Hardaway joined the Golden State Warriors in 1989, the team was coming off one of the biggest improvements in NBA history. In 1987–88, Golden State had finished with a 20–62 record. In 1988–89, the Warriors were 43–39—an improvement of twenty-three victories.

The team's coach was Don Nelson, then in his second season with the team. Before that, Nelson had been an outstanding player for the Boston Celtics, having played on five NBA championship teams. He had also coached the Milwaukee Bucks for eleven seasons, taking that team to the playoffs nine times and winning seven straight division titles.

Tim Hardaway goes up for a shot. As Golden State's point guard, Hardaway was both a good passer and a good shooter.

Nelson was immediately impressed with Hardaway. Just as he had done in grammar school, high school, and college, Hardaway had to prove that he was not too short to play the game on a high level. He proved it quickly to Nelson. "They told me I wouldn't be able to play defense, wouldn't be able to cover guys, but I was always quick enough," Hardaway said. "A lot of people counted me out real quick. That's what drove me. I'm just quick. I zoom up and down the court."[1]

When Hardaway arrived at Golden State, he was nearly grown up, but he still had a little maturing to do. He listened to Coach Nelson, and the maturation process went along rapidly. Nelson said Hardaway was adaptable and easy to coach, and he made Hardaway the Warriors' floor leader. The Warriors had veterans such as Chris Mullin and Mitch Richmond on the team, but the point guard—the lead guard on the team who always runs the offense—was Hardaway.

The three players blended together perfectly. For the next few seasons, they became known as Run TMC, for Tim, Mitch, and Chris. They turned out to be one of the most exciting and accomplished trios in the NBA. Neither Hardaway nor Richmond is with Golden State now. Tim Hardaway plays for Miami and Mitch Richmond is with the Washington

Wizards. Chris Mullin is back with the Warriors after having played for the Indiana Pacers. Even though they are no longer playing together, they are still the best of friends.

As Golden State's point guard, Tim Hardaway had the job of making the other players happy. He needed to pass the ball, to try to get everyone involved, and to act like a leader his teammates could respect.

Hardaway had a knack not only for moving the ball around, but also for scoring. That was a big plus for a player at his position. Some point guards are terrific playmakers but poor shooters. Hardaway was both a good passer and a good shooter. "He sees his time of the game when he's got to hunker down offensively," Pat Riley, Hardaway's Miami Heat coach, said. "He knows when he should be distributing the ball and other times he takes it upon himself to make plays. He'll drive, he'll kick it out, he'll pull up on the jumper, he'll mix it up."[2]

Those characteristics reminded Riley of another great player he had once coached—Earvin "Magic" Johnson—when both were with the Los Angeles Lakers. The one big difference between Johnson and Hardaway was their size. Johnson was six feet eight inches tall, Hardaway was listed at six feet—and that might have been an exaggeration by about an inch.

Hardaway accepted Riley's praise with little emotion but with much pride. "It's about knowing how to play," he said. "Knowing your strengths and weaknesses. Knowing when to go to the hole and when to pull up for a jump shot. Knowing when to take your man."[3]

In addition to beating the opposition with his line drive jump shots, Tim Hardaway dazzled them with his post-up play. Few players of his size have the ability to go down low and work in the pivot. Hardaway was not afraid. He thrived on it. Although he was small, he was muscular, at 195 pounds. "He's like a miniature Charles Barkley body down there in the post," said Danny Ainge, former coach of the Phoenix Suns and an NBA player for fourteen seasons.

> He can just outmuscle people, then he's got the great passing skills, great ball-handling skills and he's a great shooter. All those things combined make him probably the best low-post player on the Heat. Not just among point guards, but he's probably their best scorer down in the low post. As a point guard in the league, other than Magic Johnson, there's never been a better post-up player than Timmy.[4]

Hardaway did not just begin posting up when he joined the Heat in 1996. He began that practice in the pros with Golden State. Now he has perfected that move with Miami. "The reason why Tim is so good down in the post is because of his frame," former Miami forward Jamal Mashburn said.

> He's low to the ground, plus still pretty wide. So his center of gravity and balance are pretty good. He's a thick point guard. He's not small and fragile so he can go down there and post up those little guards. Tim's not a small guy. He has a big upper frame and has a big lower body.[5]

Often when Hardaway goes into the low post, he demands to be double-teamed. Then his point guard mentality comes into play, and he is able to make the right decision—pass or shoot? When he is double-teamed, he usually finds the open man for an easy shot. When he gets only single coverage, he will likely take the shot. He is confident that he can shoot the ball over anybody, with little regard for the size of the other player.

It is the idea of posting up that excites him. He likes getting down and dirty, and banging around bigger players. He enjoys showing opponents that he can take the pushing and shoving, and still make the type of play that makes something good happen for his team.

John Starks, formerly with the Knicks and then Golden State, and now with the Utah Jazz, compares Hardaway to the great Michael Jordan. Jordan led the Chicago Bulls to six NBA titles during the 1990s and is considered by many astute NBA observers to be the best to ever play the game. "He's like Michael Jordan, where he [Hardaway] has three or four moves he can go to," said Starks. "He's the type of guy who can do a lot of things with the ball. You don't try to lock in on one thing."[6]

Over the years, Hardaway has also developed into one of the game's great clutch shooters. He is always ready and willing to take the last shot when it will determine a game's outcome. "Tim is just one of the great clutch players in the game today," Danny Ainge said. "One of those guys who is physically and mentally tough, and the closer to the end of the game, the tougher he is."[7]

Sacramento forward Chris Webber has the same feeling. "He's hard-nosed, aggressive," said Webber. "I consider him like a little big man. He thinks he's a big man, a post-up guy. He thinks he is 6-10, which is good."[8]

Tim Hardaway's attitude in those late-game situations is similar to that of Indiana's Reggie Miller.

FACT

Tim Hardaway is known throughout the NBA as someone the younger players can talk to about their problems. He tells them not to take their problems home, but to leave them on the court. He also tells the younger players to always have time for their families. Tim Hardaway's immediate family includes his wife, Yolanda, and two children, son Tim, Jr. and daughter Nia.

Miller has gained a reputation within the league for hitting many big shots down the stretch. Many have come against the New York Knicks, especially from three-point range.

Tim Hardaway's friend Chris Mullin has said that when the game is on the line, Hardaway does not like to give up the ball. Hardaway has the most confidence of any player Mullin has ever seen. He also has a super-quick release, so his shot is rarely blocked.

Another notable characteristic of Hardaway's game is his crossover dribble. A crossover involves switching the dribble from one hand to another. It is usually something that coaches tell their players not to do. A player who switches hands during a dribble is in danger of having the ball stripped away by the defender. But Hardaway's crossover dribble is an established part of his game.

Still another notable part of Hardaway's game is his talking on the court. He talks to opponents, to fans, and to himself. Unlike Seattle's Gary Payton, however, Hardaway is not known as a big trash talker.

Put all those skills together and Hardaway makes an excellent package as a player. Of course, he did not have his act together when he first entered the pros. Still, he showed enough flash and dash to average 14.7 points, 8.7 assists, and 3.9 rebounds per game in his first season. Those statistics were good enough to get him selected to the NBA All-Rookie Team. He was one of two unanimous choices, along with seven feet one inch David Robinson of the San Antonio Spurs. Hardaway also received the Jack McMahon Award from his teammates as the Warriors' most inspirational player.

During the next two seasons, Hardaway's numbers improved dramatically in nearly every offensive category. In 1990–91, he averaged 22.9 points, 9.7 assists, and 4 rebounds per game. Eleven times he brought his team back from 10-point deficits to win. In 1991-92, the figures were an average of 23.4 points, 10 assists, and 3.8 rebounds per game.

He was the seventh player in NBA history to average at least 20 points and 10 assists per game. Both years, he was selected to play in the All-Star Game for the Western Conference. Both years, he was the youngest player in the game. In 1991–92, however, he had to be selected for the team by NBA commissioner David Stern, even though he had the second highest number of votes for starting guard on the West team. Magic Johnson, who was retired, was made an automatic starter, so only the guard

Tim Hardaway improved all aspects of his game during the 1991 and 1992 seasons with the Warriors.

with the most fan votes was assured of making the team. Coaches pick the reserves, and evidently they had overlooked Hardaway.

As it turned out, Johnson was named the Most Valuable Player of the 1992 game. Hardaway was also a major contributor to the West's 153–113 victory. He had 14 points and 7 assists in the West's biggest winning margin ever in the All-Star Game.

That year also was a banner season for the Warriors. The team finished with a 55–27 record, the second-highest number of victories in team history. Only the 1975–76 team, which went 59–23, had a better record. Unfortunately for Hardaway and the Warriors, the Seattle SuperSonics, who had finished eight games behind Golden State in the Pacific Division, knocked them out of the playoffs in four games in the first round.

Things began to unravel for Golden State the following year. In 1992–93, the team's four leading scorers of the previous season—Tim Hardaway, Chris Mullin, Sarunas Marciulionis, and Billy Owens—each missed several games because of injuries. Without their help, the team's record plummeted to 34–48, a decrease of twenty-five victories from the previous year. That record was not good enough for the team to make the playoffs.

When Hardaway played that season, in a total of

sixty-six games, he was very effective. He missed sixteen games because of an injured right knee. He averaged 21.5 points, 10.6 assists, and 4 rebounds, and made the All-Star Team for the third consecutive year. Again, he helped the West win, 135–132, in overtime. Hardaway contributed 16 points and 4 assists. He was hoping to get the Warriors back into the playoffs in 1993–94.

Chapter 5
Golden, Then Not So Golden

The 1993–94 season held a lot of promise for the Warriors. On draft day in 1993, they had acquired Chris Webber in a trade with the Orlando Magic. In exchange for Webber, the Warriors sent Anfernee "Penny" Hardaway, their No. 1 pick, to the Magic.

Chris Webber had been an outstanding player at Michigan. He had great leaping and shooting ability. He also could run the floor very well. His athleticism was just what the Warriors appeared to need. With Tim Hardaway, Chris Webber, Latrell Sprewell, Chris Mullin, Billy Owens, Avery Johnson, and Chris Gatling, Golden State had the makings of a team that could go far in the playoffs. As the team went to training camp, expectations were high, despite the lack of an established center on the team. Before long, the Warriors also were missing their No. 1 point guard. Less than three weeks into training camp, Tim Hardaway tore the anterior cruciate ligament (ACL) in his left knee during an exhibition game. He would be out for the rest of the season. That was a devastating blow to the team's playoff hopes. It was also a crushing injury for Hardaway. At twenty-seven, he was at the peak of his career. He was coming off three straight 20-plus scoring seasons and three consecutive appearances in the All-Star Game.

The injury not only ended his season, but also appeared to threaten his career. A torn ACL is one of the most dreaded injuries for a professional athlete. This is especially true for someone like Hardaway, who relies so heavily on speed and change of direction. "I was worried I wouldn't come back from it," Hardaway said.[1]

Hardaway was concerned about the severity of the injury, but he believed that a dedicated rehabilitation program would speed his return—if he was to return at all. Hardaway does not do things lightly, so it was no surprise that he worked diligently and for many hours each day trying to get the knee back into shape. "I knew it was going to be a long, hard road back," he said. "But I looked at Danny

Manning. I looked at Mark Price. I said, 'Hey, if they made it back from ACL injuries, how come I can't?'"[2]

Manning had injured a knee in his first season in the NBA with the Los Angeles Clippers, in 1988–89. Price had been injured during the 1990–91 season, in his fifth year with the Cleveland Cavaliers. Both returned the following season, to play more than seventy games each. That gave Hardaway hope.

Surprisingly, the Warriors flourished without their star playmaker. The team made a remarkable improvement from the previous season, going 50–32. That was sixteen more victories than in 1992–93. Their record got them into the playoffs. They did not stay for long, however. The Phoenix Suns knocked them out in the first round, winning three straight games. That was not long enough for Hardaway to return to action. Had the Warriors advanced to the Western Conference Finals, there was a chance that Hardaway could have played. He had made a quicker recovery than expected. "I was with them and I tried to help as much as I could, but there was only so much I could do," he said. "I was treated like an outsider. It hurt, but I could understand."[3]

The year away from the game was the most challenging of Hardaway's life. He could handle the

FACT

Tim Hardaway runs summer camps for kids in Chicago, Illinois, and El Paso, Texas. He also is co-founder of an organization in Chicago called The Support Group. It offers educational assistance to needy children. He returns to Chicago every summer to be the host of a black-tie fundraiser.

physical rehabilitation, but not the mental part of it. He wondered whether he could come back. If he came back, would he be as good a player as before?

His family boosted his spirits. They urged him to return. With their support, his attitude changed. "I have dealt with adversity from Day 1," Hardaway said. "In grammar school, high school and college, I was too short. A lot of people counted me out real quick. A lot of people gave up on me [after the injury]. They didn't think I would get back. That was a motivational tool for me."[4]

After not being able to rejoin the team in 1993–94, Hardaway was anxious to begin the 1994–95 season. Despite the playoff disappointment, the Warriors had built a winning attitude the previous year, and Hardaway wanted to be an important part of the team. Golden State had become a high-scoring team, averaging 107.9 points per game, second highest in the league. With Hardaway, that average had the potential to increase. He was an efficient point producer and a pinpoint passer.

Unfortunately for the Warriors, that optimism was never realized. Chris Webber did not report to camp. He exercised the one-year out option in his contract. He wanted to be traded. The Warriors reluctantly gave in. They sent Webber to the Washington Wizards in exchange for Tom Gugliotta.

After sitting out with a knee injury in 1993–94, Hardaway hoped to help the team improve during the 1994–95 season.

Webber had been a vital part of the Warriors' offense. He was their second leading scorer, with 17.5 points per game, and their leading rebounder at 9.1. He was also the league's Rookie of the Year. In Gugliotta, the Warriors got a good scorer but a player with little speed. That would mean a change in the offensive flow. Instead of moving the ball up the court quickly and beating the opposition down the floor, they would operate more slowly.

Even without Webber, Hardaway was optimistic, however. "We still need a big man to help us down low," said Hardaway, "but I feel we can win it all. We just have to play harder and better."[5]

The results were disastrous. The Warriors got off to a horrible start and did not recover over the course of the season. Losing created discontent among the players. The unhappiness boiled over into the locker room. The team's poor play bothered Hardaway. He became so angry that he got into a series of arguments with backcourt partner Latrell Sprewell.

After reaching a truce with Sprewell, Hardaway had an even uglier disagreement with Rick Adelman. Adelman had replaced Don Nelson as coach in midseason. The rift between Adelman and Hardaway led to a benching for Hardaway. Once given free rein by Nelson, Hardaway was now a reserve. He was replaced in the starting lineup by B. J. Armstrong, who lacked both Hardaway's scoring ability and his passing skills. As Armstong struggled, so did the Warriors.

It was the first time in Hardaway's NBA career that he did not start a game in which he was available to play. He later said he would accept a reserve role as long as the team won and he could help.

His communication with Adelman never improved, but Hardaway did not let his feelings affect his play. He played in sixty-two games that season and averaged 20.1 points and 9.3 assists. He missed the final twenty games of the season after having surgery to repair a torn ligament in his left wrist. The Warriors ended the 1994–95 season with an embarrassing 26–56 record, twenty-four fewer victories than the team had recorded the previous year.

The 1995–96 season did not start much better for the Warriors, or for Hardaway. He asked to be traded. Two-thirds of the way through the season, the Warriors gave Tim Hardaway his wish. They traded him to the Miami Heat, along with forward Chris Gatling. In exchange, Golden State received center Kevin Willis and guard Bimbo Coles.

Hardaway was delighted with the trade. He was happy to be playing for Pat Riley, one of the game's

FACT

Hardaway twice tied a single-game NBA playoff record for most steals, with 8. He did it against the Los Angeles Lakers on May 8, 1991 and on April 30, 1992 against the Seattle SuperSonics.

Tim Hardaway shows his intensity on the court. As a member of the Miami Heat, Hardaway would use that intensity to help the team make it to the playoffs.

most respected coaches. He was ready for a mental rejuvenation. With Riley, Hardaway felt the Heat would be a playoff team and even have a chance to win the league championship. Riley had earned championship rings with the Los Angeles Lakers as a player in 1972, as an assistant with the Lakers in 1980, and as the team's head coach in 1982, 1985, 1987, and 1988. Four other times as head coach, he had taken his teams to the NBA Finals. That was what Hardaway wanted, just a chance to get to the championship round. Then, maybe, he would earn a title, and a championship ring.

Chapter 6
Heating Up in Miami

On the same day that Miami acquired Tim Hardaway and Chris Gatling from Golden State, Pat Riley arranged two other deals. In one trade, he got forwards Walt Williams and Tyrone Corbin from Sacramento in exchange for forward Billy Owens and guard Kevin Gamble. In the other, he received guard Tony Smith from Phoenix in exchange for guard Terrence Rencher. In addition, Riley signed veteran guard Jeff Malone to a second ten-day contract.

At the time, the Heat were floundering. Their record was 24–29 and they were in danger of missing the playoffs. This was Riley's fourteenth season as a head coach in the NBA, and his teams had never failed to reach the postseason. None of his previous teams in Los Angeles and New York had won fewer than fifty games. Now it appeared that his team would have trouble reaching forty victories.

He hoped the addition of the new talent on the day of the NBA trading deadline would energize the Heat. Of all the newcomers, Hardaway was the key. He would run the offense and be counted upon to combine with center Alonzo Mourning for much of the team's scoring. Hardaway also tried to be the inspirational leader. He encouraged the players to talk to each other frequently and to become like a family. That, he felt, would make for better team play.

It did. After splitting their first six games following Hardaway's arrival, the Heat won eight of their next nine. That put them over the .500 mark, with a 35–33 record. The winning spurt helped Miami make the playoffs. The Heat finished with a 42–40 record, matching the best record in the team's history. The Heat finished one game ahead of Charlotte, for the final playoff spot in the Eastern Conference.

Miami did not last long in the playoffs, however. In the first round, the Heat had the unenviable task of facing the Chicago Bulls. The Bulls, in Michael Jordan's first season back from playing baseball, had compiled a 72–10 record, the best in NBA history.

The Miami Heat acquired Tim Hardaway from the Warriors on February 22, 1996. Coach Pat Riley hoped that Hardaway would run the offense and work with center Alonzo Mourning to score points for the team.

Chicago overwhelmed the Heat in three games, winning by margins of 17, 31, and 21 points. Hardaway could not be blamed for the opening-game loss. He set a franchise playoff record, with 30 points.

This was the first time a team coached by Riley had not won a game in the postseason. Riley vowed that would not happen again in the 1996–97 season. During the off-season, he signed several free agents, including forward P. J. Brown, guards Voshon Lenard and Dan Majerle, and center Isaac Austin. He also extended Alonzo Mourning's contract and re-signed Hardaway, who was a free agent.

Hardaway, however, was not happy with the circumstances surrounding his signing. He felt Riley had slighted him by first talking to several other point guards. When Riley finally came back to Hardaway, he signed for $13 million over four years. With incentives, he could make as much as $18 million. Still, he took a $1 million pay cut from his previous contract. By most people's standards, that still was an extraordinary deal. As an NBA player of great talent, though, Hardaway felt shortchanged.

He agreed to the contract because he wanted to remain in Miami and play under Riley. As a free agent, Hardaway could have earned more money. He was contacted by the New York Knicks, Houston

Rockets, and Denver Nuggets. He rejected all of their offers. He craved team success and felt Miami held the most appeal. In order to fit within the salary structure of the team, he accepted less money than he had made the year before. He called his gesture a sacrifice. "I understand that and I made sure Pat [Riley] understood that," Hardaway said.[1]

As the 1996–97 season approached, Tim Hardaway was eager to get going. "I feel the same as I did five years ago," he said. "My weight is down. My knee is stronger. I knew I had to get out of Golden State in order to be my old self again. . . . When I got here [Miami], it was just The Guy [Riley] putting the ball in my hands saying, 'Run my team.' I was like, 'All right, let's go.' I had lots of fun last year. I'm going to have more fun this year."[2]

Riley enjoyed having Hardaway on the Heat. He especially liked his attitude. Tim Hardaway had a no-nonsense approach on the court, the kind that is necessary for a winning atmosphere. "I think he likes being in a program that isn't going to waste his time, that is structured and disciplined," Riley said. "He is serious about winning."[3]

Hardaway will do almost anything to win. "When the game is on the line, you have to wrestle him for the ball," said former Golden State

FACT

Pat Riley of the Miami Heat has coached in more playoff games than anyone else in NBA history. He has also won and lost the most playoff games.

teammate, Chris Mullin. "He's got the most confidence I've ever seen in a human being."[4]

In the locker room, Tim Hardaway is a different person. Much of the laughter there comes from his part of the room. He smiles often and thoroughly enjoys himself. He also enjoyed himself on the court during the 1996–97 season. The Heat got off to a terrific start and won consistently through the entire season. Even though they were winning, Riley was not completely satisfied. With the team's record at 38–12, he made a major move to help the team for the rest of the season and in the playoffs. Realizing the Heat needed more scoring punch to complement Hardaway and Mourning, Riley made a deal with the Dallas Mavericks. In the trade, Riley acquired high-scoring forward Jamal Mashburn. In return, he sent to Dallas guards Sasha Danilovic and Martin Muursepp, and forward Kurt Thomas. The deal gave Miami a strong three-pronged attack. Opposing teams would have a great deal of difficulty trying to stop the Heat's offense. Not many were successful. Miami finished with a 61–21 record. That was the best in the team's history, and it gave the Heat their first Atlantic Division title. Hardaway was the catalyst. He had led the team in scoring with a 20.3 average, in assists with an 8.6 average, in steals with 151, and in minutes played

Hardaway goes up for a shot. The 1996–97 season brought an Atlantic Division title to Hardaway and the Heat.

with a team-record 3,136. He set a career high with 45 points in a game against Washington. He also was selected to play in the All-Star Game for the fourth time. In fourteen minutes, he scored 10 points in the East's 132–120 victory.

As division champions, the Heat got the home court advantage in the first round of the playoffs. They took full advantage of that benefit. They played the Orlando Magic and beat them, three games to two. The Heat won all three games at home, while the Magic won both games at Orlando. Next up were the New York Knicks. The Heat was a team playing only its ninth season in the league. The Knicks had been around since 1946. Still, the teams had built up a heated rivalry. Each game between them had become like a battle in a war. Much of the fierce competition between them had developed because of Pat Riley. Before joining the Heat in 1995, he had coached the Knicks for four years. By the time he left New York for Miami, Riley had rebuilt the Knicks into a powerful team. The organization felt, however, that he had deserted it just as New York was on the brink of winning the NBA Championship.

Miami, of course, was delighted to have a coach of Riley's stature. Now the Heat was the better team. They had finished four games ahead of the Knicks in the division. That gave the Heat home court advantage again in the Eastern Conference Semifinals.

The Knicks overcame that advantage for Miami and swung it in their favor by winning Game 1, 88–79. New York's Allan Houston led all scorers with 27 points, and teammate Patrick Ewing had 24. Hardaway topped Miami with 21, one more than Mourning. The winning team also had 88 points in Game 2, but this time it was Miami, winning 88–84. Hardaway was by far the game's outstanding player. He broke his Heat playoff record with a game-high 34 points, including thirteen straight Miami points during one stretch. He also had 8 rebounds and 4 assists.

In New York for Game 3, the Knicks regained the advantage, winning 77–73, with the help of Patrick Ewing's 25 points. New York took what appeared to be a commanding 3–1 lead in the series by winning Game 4, 89–76. John Starks came off the bench to score 21 points in the winning effort.

Hardaway was not his usual productive self in either of those games. His shooting had gone into a funk. In Game 3, he hit only six of twenty-two shots from the floor, and in Game 4, he was four for ten.

Then came the pivotal Game 5 at the Miami Arena. The Knicks needed only one more victory to eliminate the Heat and advance to the Eastern

Conference Finals against the Chicago Bulls. The Bulls were waiting for the winner of the New York-Miami series. They already had beaten the Atlanta Hawks in five games in their second-round series.

The pressure was on the Heat. They were playing before a sellout crowd of 14,782. They did not want to be embarrassed by losing the series at home. They did not want to be beaten by the Knicks. They had to win or be shamed. The game was close until the fourth quarter. Then, the Heat went on a 17–2 run and took control. The Knicks, confident they would end the series, became frustrated. With less than two minutes remaining, New York's Charlie Ward undercut P.J. Brown after the Miami forward converted a free throw. Brown fought back by throwing Ward hard to the floor.

Then came the brawl that led to the ejection of Charlie Ward and John Starks (for the Knicks), and P. J. Brown (for Miami). Miami was in command and went on to win, 96–81.

Charlie Ward, Patrick Ewing, and Allan Houston were missing from Game 6 for the Knicks, and P. J. Brown was missing for the Heat. They were all suspended for the contest at Madison Square Garden. For Miami, Brown's loss was insignificant, compared to the losses for the Knicks. Ewing, Houston, Starks, and Johnson were New York's top

Hardaway goes up for a shot as Knicks defenders look on. The rivalry between the two teams is legendary.

scorers and Ward was the team's No. 2 point guard. Brown, though a tireless player, was primarily a defensive specialist and rebounder.

Going into the fourth quarter of Game 6, the Knicks were clinging to a two-point lead. They had few players who could come off the bench. As a result, four of their players were forced to play forty minutes or more and they finally wilted. Miami rallied, winning 95–90. That tied the series 3-3 and forced a decisive Game 7.

Again the Knicks would be more shorthanded than the Heat. That was not the best of circumstances for the Knicks, who would be coming into Miami's arena. After all, Miami had survived two possible elimination games and now had renewed confidence.

The Heat bolted to a 49–32 halftime lead against the Knicks. In the third quarter, Mourning sat on the bench with his fourth personal foul, and New York cut Miami's lead to 55–47. Hardaway then took over the game single-handedly. When the quarter was over, Miami's lead had been restored to seventeen points, 71–54.

New York went on its biggest scoring binge of the series in the fourth quarter, collecting 36 points, but it was not nearly enough. Miami went on to win easily, 101–90.

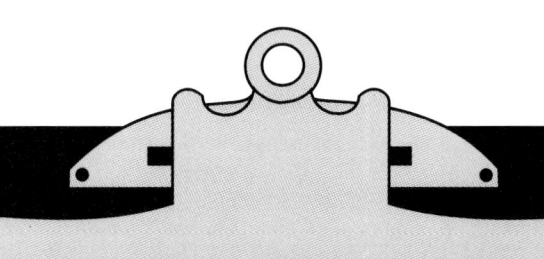

STATS

League Leaders in Three-Pointers Made

Tim Hardaway ranked first in the league as of the middle of January 2001 in three-point shots made. The league's top ten three-point shooters as of January 2001 are listed here.

Player	TEAM	PCT	ATT	MADE
1. Tim Hardaway	Miami	.363	259	94
2. Ray Allen	Milwaukee	.413	208	86
3. Reggie Miller	Indiana	.373	201	75
4. Vince Carter	Toronto	.433	171	74
5. Dick Nowitzki	Dallas	.403	181	73
6. Antoine Walker	Boston	.355	200	71
7. Voshon Lenard	Denver	.389	180	70
8. Lindsey Hunter	Milwaukee	.392	176	69
9. (tied) Rashard Lewis	Seattle	.430	142	61
10. (tied) Nick Van Exel	Denver	.337	181	61

Tim Hardaway is a hard worker who always gives his all on the court.

Tim Hardaway finished the game with 38 points, a playoff career high and a franchise record. He had risen to the occasion when the Heat needed him most. That was the kind of gutsy performance they were expecting when they acquired him from Golden State.

Talking after the game, Hardaway said,

> I was hyped. I came out and started making shots. I can't remember having a quarter [the third] like that in the NBA. I was in a zone. I was having fun out there, doing my thing, going to the hole, shooting threes.[5]

Miami guard Willie Anderson was impressed but not surprised by Hardaway's sensational showing. "What Tim did you don't get to see often as a player, a spectator, or a journalist," said Anderson.

> When you do see it, it lasts a lifetime. Tim has been shooting that way all his life. All he needs is a little space to get his shot airborne. You know when he makes one, he's going to make another and another.[6]

That was just what he did against the helpless Knicks.

Even the Knicks were impressed. As much as they disliked the Heat, they all hugged Hardaway after the game. It was a fitting tribute to a great athlete who had had a great game.

Chapter 7
Tim Hardaway Is In Charge

Tim Hardaway's magnificent game against the Knicks established him as a true hero in Miami. Hardaway was not yet in the same league as Reggie Miller of the Indiana Pacers, who had burned the Knicks more often than Hardaway. Still, Hardaway was a player New York did not want to see on the court, and the Knicks were a team Hardaway disliked playing more than any other. Off the court was another matter.

On the court, the desire to win is foremost. Hardaway's intense desire to beat the Knicks—and every other team—is evident in every game he plays. That desire to win is what Coach Riley likes so much about him and it explains why he designated Hardaway the team's floor leader. "He's my leader," Riley said of Hardaway. "He's our leader. I have total trust and faith in him."[1]

That was the same way Riley felt about one of his great players on the Los Angeles Lakers. "He's the closest to anybody I've coached to being like Magic Johnson," Riley said. "He's a six foot Magic Johnson is what he is. He can shoot, he can pass, post up, and he's a leader."[2]

Riley also compared Hardaway to another great player. "Tim to us is like Michael Jordan to Chicago," he said. "When the game is on the line, he can be heroic."[3] While Riley put Hardaway in charge on the floor, he had to make sure Hardaway did not get out of control. At times, he got too carried away with the emotion of a game and his play suffered. Occasionally he would veer from the game plan, so it was Riley's job to keep a tight rein on him. "He can embrace the competition," Riley said. "What he has to embrace is the game plan."[4]

Hardaway has always understood Riley's position. The problem is that Tim Hardaway plays the game with such confidence and fervor that sometimes he does not realize he is playing out of control. Sometimes he sees teammates struggling and then decides to take over. At those times, he may take an ill-advised three-pointer in transition, a play that

Tim Hardaway moves around the court with ease. Coach Riley has compared Tim Hardaway's importance to the Heat to that of Michael Jordan for the Bulls.

disrupts Miami's offensive flow. Riley gets upset at those kind of shots and lets Hardaway know of his displeasure.

Hardaway shrugs off the criticism, because he knows Riley is as serious about winning as he is. Both are fierce competitors, and sometimes their emotions boil over in the heat of a game. The respect they have for each other, though, does not suffer. Both want to win so badly that each loss is like a personal affront.

Riley does not lose faith in Hardaway, even when he is having a bad game. Riley knows Hardaway's capabilities and has seen him come through often under pressure. Riley trusts Hardaway more than he does most players. "In certain game situations, he puts it all on his shoulders," teammate Alonzo Mourning said of Hardaway.

> He wants to make the plays. He wants to take the big shots. We're so used to it now because he's done it the past couple of years. It's by instinct now and we all expect it of him. . . . He's pretty much established himself as the one that's going to take the big shot. So be it. The rest of us just have to do our jobs.[5]

After beating the Knicks with that magnificent comeback from a deficit of three games to one in the 1997 playoffs, the Heat faced their old nemesis, the

Tim Hardaway is a fierce competitor who can play well under pressure.

Chicago Bulls, with Michael Jordan. Chicago had swept the Heat in three games in both the 1992 and 1996 playoffs, both times in the first round. Now they were meeting for the Eastern Conference Championship.

The last team to come back from a three-to-one playoff deficit—the Houston Rockets—had won the NBA title in 1995. The Rockets overcame the Phoenix Suns in the Western Conference Semifinals. That fact made Hardaway and the Heat feel confident. "Nobody expected us to be here," Hardaway said. "Now we're going to have some more people doubting us. Well, we can beat anybody."[6]

A year earlier, however, Hardaway had predicted the Heat would beat the Bulls and the results were disastrous. Michael Jordan, who had averaged 45 points against Miami in 1992 and 30 points against the Heat four years later, again outplayed them. This time, Jordan averaged 30.1 points, and Chicago eliminated the Heat in five games. Hardaway, apparently drained from the New York series, played poorly in the first three games, and Miami lost each game. Hardaway recovered to score 25 points in Game 4 and Miami won, prolonging the series. Hardaway again led the Heat with 27 points in Game 5, but the Bulls won, clinching the series.

> **FACT**
>
> On October 29, 1997, in South Dade County in Florida, Tim Hardaway and the Heat's coach, Pat Riley, wore hard hats and hoisted cinder blocks into place over wet cement. They were helping build a new $8 million assistance center for the homeless. It was part of the Heat's Team Up Day, an NBA program that supports community projects in league cities.

Miami was right back in the playoffs in 1998, after having finished first in the Atlantic Division.

Who would be waiting for them in the first round? None other than the New York Knicks. "We really want the Knicks," Hardaway said. "And they really want us. They're confident they can take us down. That's insulting, but it's OK because we can take them down, too."[7]

The Heat appeared to have a huge advantage over New York. They had finished twelve games ahead of the Knicks during the regular season, and New York was without its star center, Patrick Ewing. Ewing had torn ligaments in his right wrist during a game against Milwaukee and had played only twenty-six games during the regular season. Without Ewing, New York was only 28–28. Their chances against Miami appeared slim, and the oddsmakers made the Heat heavy favorites.

The oddsmakers took a beating. So did the Heat. After splitting the first four games, the Knicks overcame the absence of suspended players Larry Johnson and Chris Mills in addition to a 21-point performance by Hardaway in Game 5 to win, 98–81. The Heat were also without two key players, Mourning (who was suspended) and Dan Majerle (who had a groin injury). Nothing could excuse another bitter defeat for Hardaway and the Heat.

The loss of Alonzo Mourning (front right), who was suspended after a fight in Game 4, was a tremendous blow for the Heat in 1998 against the New York Knicks.

Johnson, Mills, and Mourning all had been suspended for fighting at the end of Game 4. Although the Heat lost only one player (Mourning) to the Knicks' two (Johnson and Mills), Miami appeared to be more affected by the suspensions, because Mourning was the only player on the Heat who could be effective on defense against Patrick Ewing. Miami's shooting was the worst of the series. The teams met in 1999 for the third consecutive time in the playoffs. Again Miami was the overwhelming favorite. After all, the team had finished with the best record in the Eastern Conference in a season shortened to fifty games by the NBA lockout. The Heat were the No. 1 seeds in the East.

The Knicks barely made the playoffs, qualifying eighth, and last. Never had a No. 8 team beaten a No. 1 team in the Eastern Conference playoffs. The Knicks then became the first, by the barest of margins. Surprisingly, none of the first four games was close. New York won the first, 95–73, Miami the second, 83–73, New York the third, 97–73, and Miami the fourth, 87–72.

Game 5 turned out to be one of the most dramatic in playoff history. The game swayed back and forth most of the way, with neither team gaining a substantial advantage. In the final minute, the Heat were clinging to a 77–76 lead and had possession of

Tim Hardaway goes up for an easy shot—with no opposing players in sight.

the ball. They put the ball into the hands of Hardaway, usually their most dependable player.

Hardaway started to drive toward the basket. He got into the lane. He started to go up with the ball. And then . . . it was gone. Twenty-four and nine-tenths seconds remained in the game. "I just lost it," said Hardaway. "I was trying to make a jump pass to Terry Porter and it slipped out of my hands. Man, it just hurts. It was the right play. I was open. I drove. It slipped."[8] The ball slipped right into the hands of the Knicks, who immediately called a time-out. When play resumed and the final frantic seconds ticked away, the Knicks missed a couple of shots. Then they got the ball to Allan Houston.

Houston drove toward the basket and put up a finger roll. The ball hit the glass backboard and hung on the rim agonizingly before dropping through the hoop. Only eight-tenths of a second remained. It was too late for the Heat to do anything, and when the game ended, 78–77, in New York's favor, the Knicks celebrated wildly. The downhearted Heat walked slowly to their dressing room, pondering another bitter defeat to their rivals.

The most discouraged player was Tim Hardaway. Not only had he made the bad play in the final minute that allowed the Knicks to get the ball; he had had the poorest playoff series of his

Tim Hardaway appears to defy the laws of gravity. He is guarded by Kenyon Martin of the Nets.

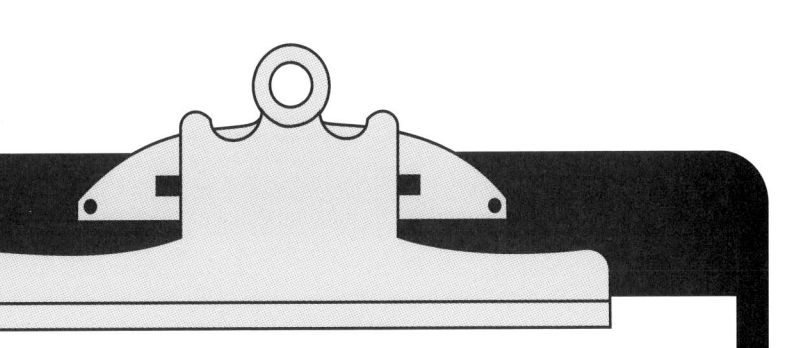

STATS

League Leaders in Free-Throw Percentage

Tim Hardaway ranked thirteenth in the league in free-throw percentage as of the beginning of December 2000. The league's top fifteen free-throw shooters are shown here.

PLAYER	TEAM	FTM	FTA	FT%
1. Jalen Rose	Indiana	29	30	.967
2. Darrell Armstrong	Orlando	42	45	.933
3. Reggie Miller	Indiana	82	89	.921
4. Chauncey Billups	Minnesota	68	74	.919
5. Steve Nash	Dallas	55	60	.917
6. Jim Jackson	Atlanta	62	68	.912
7. Terrell Brandon	Minnesota	39	43	.907
8. (tied) Ray Allen	Milwaukee	83	92	.902
8. (tied) Steve Francis	Houston	74	82	.902
10. (tied) Doug Christie	Sacramento	25	28	.893
10. (tied) Rashard Lewis	Seattle	50	56	.893
12. Allan Houston	New York	74	83	.892
13. (tied) Tim Hardaway	Miami	41	46	.891
13. (tied) Bryant Smith	Boston	57	64	.891
15. Kobe Bryant	L.A. Lakers	121	136	.890

career. In the five games, he shot only .268, while averaging a mere 8.8 points per game. "I let my team down by turning over the ball," he said. "It just hurts. Bad."[9]

It was one of the worst times in Hardaway's career. Still, Riley did not lose faith in him. The coach tried to comfort him, assuring Hardaway that he would continue to be the team's leader on the court. This true sign of admiration and respect was all Tim Hardaway could ask for at such a discouraging time. Riley's kind words would make Hardaway's summer vacation a little more bearable. Hardaway vowed to come back the following season even more determined to win the league title. He desperately wanted that NBA Championship ring, the crowning achievement in his otherwise outstanding career.

The Heat won the Atlantic Division title for the fourth consecutive season in 1999–2000, this time with a 52–30 record. However, they again came up short in the playoffs, leaving them still seeking that elusive championship ring.

In the first round of the playoffs, Miami swept the Detroit Pistons 3–0. Then they faced their perennial rivals, the New York Knicks, in the Eastern Conference Semifinals. This turned into another exciting and bitterly fought series.

After five games, Miami led 3–2. The Heat appeared headed toward another victory in Game 6 when they led by eighteen points, 43–25, in the second quarter. But the Knicks rallied and kept whittling away at the Miami lead. New York finally tied the score 70–70 with one and one-half minutes remaining on two free throws by Chris Childs. The Knicks won the game 72–70 on Allan Houston's pair of foul shots with 17.6 seconds left.

That set up the decisive seventh game at Miami. New York again fell behind early, trailing by as many as eleven points in the first half. As in Game 6, the Knicks made another big comeback, and they won 83–82 on Patrick Ewing's dunk shot with 1:20 to play.

Miami's Game 7 loss could not be pinned on Tim Hardaway. After missing the Detroit series with injuries, he had his best game of the playoffs in the finale against New York, scoring 15 points and handing out 7 assists. Still, that was not a very satisfying performance for Hardaway. Including the playoffs, he did not have a productive season, as the championship ring escaped him again.

During the regular season, Hardaway missed thirty games because of injuries to his left foot and right knee. He finished with career lows in scoring average (13.4) and field goal shooting percentage

(.386). In the seven playoff games against New York, he also averaged a career low in points (7.7), while shooting a pitiful .294.

Hardaway's misfortunes turned around during the summer of 2000 when he earned a gold medal as a member of the U.S. Olympic team at Sydney, Australia. The abbreviated good luck did not transfer to the Heat for the 2000–2001 season, however.

During the offseason, Coach Riley had revamped the team with a series of moves to give Alonzo Mourning and Hardaway their most talented supporting cast yet. The deals resulted in the additions of forward Anthony Mason, center-forward Brian Grant and three-time All-Star guard Eddie Jones. Mason and Jones came to Miami from the Charlotte Hornets in a nine-player trade.

Brian Grant was acquired from the Portland Trail Blazers in a three-team deal after signing a seven-year, $86 million contract. What wrecked the plan was a kidney disorder that sidelined Mourning for the entire season and threatened to end his basketball career. That left the Heat without a legitimate, proven center. Grant had played the position on occasion with Portland, but was not a bonafide center. His best position was power forward.

Alonzo Mourning's absence left Hardaway as

the only returning starter in the Miami lineup, since reserve Duane Causewell opened the season at center, along with Mason, Grant and Jones in the lineup. Hardaway, hobbled by injuries the two previous seasons, was forced to settle for a one-year contract for the 2000–2001 season. Nevertheless, he was considered the key player for the Heat. Just as he had been in the past.

Chapter Notes

Chapter 1. The Game

1. Dan LeBatard, "Hardaway Wants Beautiful Feeling," *Miami Herald*, April 18, 1998, sports, pp. 1–2.

2. D. L. Cummings, "Hardaway Gives It to Childs," *New York Daily News*, May 6, 1997, p. 75.

3. Dan Garcia, "Hardaway Won't Do a Fadeaway vs. Knicks," *The Star Ledger* (Newark, N.J.), May 6, 1997, p. 42.

4. Michael Mayo, "Hardaway Helps Knicks Go South—He Heads West," *Sun-Sentinel* (Fort Lauderdale, Fla.), May 6, 1997, p. 1C.

5. Steve Wine, Associated Press electronic press release, "Heat 101, Knicks 90," May 19, 1997.

6. Ibid.

7. Mayo, p. 1C.

8. Ibid., p. 10C.

9. Ira Winderman, "Hardaway, 3-pointers Shoot Down the Knicks," *Sun-Sentinel* (Fort Lauderdale, Fla.) May 19, 1997, p. 10C.

10. Dan LeBatard, "Heat Tops Knicks After a Wild Ride," *Miami Herald*, May 19, 1997, p. 4A.

11. Winderman, p. 10C.

12. Mayo, p. 10C.

Chapter 2. Growing Up in Chicago

1. Dan Garcia, "Hard Life Made Hardaway Star," *The Star-Ledger* (Newark, N.J.), April 23, 1997, p. 44.

2. Ira Winderman, "Like His Game, Hardaway Remains an Upbeat Force," *Sun-Sentinel* (Fort Lauderdale, Fla.), October 1, 1996, p. 6.

3. Amy Shipley, "Can't Forgive, Can't Forget," *Miami Herald*, February 7, 1997, p. 8D.

4. Shipley, p. 7D

5. Garcia, p. 44.

6. Ibid.

7. Shipley, p. 7D.

Chapter 3. High School and College

1. Holden Lewis, "Chicago Fire," Associated Press electronic press release, March 12, 1988.

2. Basketball Hall of Fame press release, April 15, 1989.

3. Derry Eads, "Hardaway: 'Knuckleballer' Outsmarts Foes," *El Paso Herald Post*, February 18, 1987, p. 32.

4. Ibid.

5. Lewis, Associated Press electronic press release.

6. Ibid.

7. Steve Almond, "Hardaway," *El Paso Times*, March 1, 1990, p. 21.

8. S. L. Price, "Hot Hand," *Sports Illustrated*, April 30, 1997, p. 30.

9. Ibid.

10. Amy Shipley, "Can't Forgive, Can't Forget," *Miami Herald*, February 7, 1997, p. 7D.

Chapter 4. Turning Pro

1. Amy Shipley, "The Fast Lane," *Miami Herald*, December 4, 1996, p. 1D.

2. Steve Wyche, "Magic in a Smaller Bottle," *Miami Herald*, January 1, 1998, p. 1D.

3. Ibid.

4. Robes Patton, "For a 6-Foot Point Guard, Tim Hardaway Is One of the League's Best Post-Up Men," *Sun-Sentinel* (Fort Lauderdale, Fla.), February 9, 1998, sports, p. 1.

5. Ibid.

6. Tom D'Angelo, "Hardaway Knows Where He Ought to Be," *Palm Beach Post* (Palm Beach, Fla.), February 7, 1998, sports, p. 1.

7. Ibid.

8. Russ Bengston, "Tim Hardaway's Game Almost Drowns Out His Voice," *Slam*, October 1, 1997, p. 38.

Chapter 5. Golden, Then Not So Golden

1. Amy Shipley, "The Fast Lane," *Miami Herald*, December 4, 1996, p. 6D.

2. Ira Winderman, "Like His Game, Hardaway Remains an Upbeat Force," *Sun-Sentinel* (Fort Lauderdale, Fla.), October 1, 1996, p. 6.

3. David DuPree, "Tim Hardaway Can Do It All Again After Injury Layoff," *USA Today*, October 11, 1994, p. 7.

4. Dan Garcia, "Hard Life Made Hardaway Star," *The Star-Ledger* (Newark, N.J.), April 23, 1997, p. 5D.

5. DuPree, p. 7.

Chapter 6. Heating Up in Miami

1. Robes Patton, "Hardaway Goes With Low Bid," *Sun-Sentinel* (Fort Lauderdale, Fla.), July 27, 1996, p. 6.

2. Amy Shipley, "The Fast Lane," *Miami Herald*, October 4, 1996, p. 6D.

3. Ibid.

4. Russ Bengtson, "Tim Hardaway's Game Almost Drowns Out His Voice," *Slam*, October 1, 1997, p. 38.

5. Roscoe Nance, "Hardaway Heats Up Against Knicks," *USA Today*, May 19, 1997, p. 5C.

6. Ibid.

Chapter 7. Tim Hardaway Is In Charge

1. Don Burke, "The Penalty Against Hardaway," *The Star-Ledger* (Newark, N.J.), May 15, 1999, p. 54.

2. Greg Boeck, "Hardaway Shows He Can Handle Heat Attack," *USA Today*, September 20, 1997, p. 5C.

3. Darren Everson, "Tim Often Is a Hero on a Roll," *New York Daily News*, April 24, 1998, p. 83.

4. Ibid.

5. Stephen A. Smith, "Hardaway Is Key to Knicks-Heat Series," *Philadelphia Inquirer*, April 24, 1998, p. 35.

6. Steve Wyche, "N.Y. Knocked Out, Heat Looks to Bulls," *Miami Herald*, May 19, 1997, p. 1D.

7. Dan LeBatard, "Hardaway Wants 'Beautiful' Feeling," *Miami Herald*, April 18, 1998, p. 1D.

8. Fred Kerber, "Tim's Turnover a Killer," *New York Post*, May 20, 1999, p. 71.

9. Ibid., p. 68.

Career Statistics

YEAR	TEAM	GP	FG%	REB	AST	STL	BLK	PTS	PPG
1989–90	Golden State	79	.471	310	689	165	12	1,162	14.7
1990–91	Golden State	82	.476	332	793	214	12	1,881	22.9
1991–92	Golden State	81	.461	310	807	164	13	1,893	23.4
1992–93	Golden State	66	.447	263	699	116	12	1,419	21.5
1993–94	Did not play—knee injury							
1994–95	Golden State	62	.427	190	578	88	12	1,247	20.1
1995–96	G.S.-Miami	80	.422	229	640	132	17	1,217	15.2
1996–97	Miami	81	.415	277	695	151	9	1,644	20.3
1997–98	Miami	81	.431	299	672	136	16	1,528	18.9
1998–99	Miami	48	.400	152	352	57	6	835	17.4
1999–2000	Miami	52	.386	150	385	49	4	696	13.4
TOTALS		712	.439	2,512	6,310	1,272	113	13,522	19.0

GP—Games Played
FG%—Field Goal Percentage
REB—Rebounds
AST—Assists
STL—Steals
BLK—Blocked Shots
PTS—Points Scored
PPG—Points per Game

Where to Write Tim Hardaway

Mr. Tim Hardaway
c/o Miami Heat
SunTrust International Center
One Southeast 3rd Avenue,
Suite 2300
Miami, FL. 33131

On the Internet at

The Official NBA Web site
<http://www.nba.com/playerfile/tim_hardaway.html>

Tim Hardaway's Official Web site
<http://www.timhardaway.com>

Index

A
Adelman, Rick, 56–57
Ainge, Danny, 43, 45
Anderson, Willie, 75
Archibald, Lynn, 33
Archibald, Nate, 34, 37
Armstrong, B.J., 57
Austin, Isaac, 17, 64

B
Barkley, Charles, 43
Boston Celtics, 34, 39
Brown, P.J., 8, 12–13, 17, 64, 70, 72

C
Carver High School, 20, 29
Causewell, Duane, 93
Charlotte Hornets, 62
Chicago Bulls, 19–20, 44, 62, 64, 70, 78, 82
Childs, Chris, 9, 16
Cincinnati Royals, 37
Cleveland Cavaliers, 53
Coles, Bimbo, 57
Corbin, Tyrone, 61
Cummings, Terry, 20

D
Dallas Mavericks, 66
Danilovic, Sasha, 66
Davis, Antonio, 33
Denver Nuggets, 65

E
Eubanks, Minnie E., 21–22
Ewing, Patrick, 10, 12–13, 17, 69–70, 83, 85

G
Gamble, Kevin, 61

Gatling, Chris, 51, 57, 61
Golden State Warriors, 37, 39–44, 47, 49, 51–54, 56–57, 65, 75
Grant, Brian, 92, 93
Gugliotta, Tom, 56

H
Hardaway, Anfernee, 51
Hardaway, Donald, 22, 29, 35, 37
Hardaway, Tim
  awarded Frances Pomeroy Naismith Memorial Hall of Fame Award, 32
  college at University of Texas-El Paso, 30–35
  elementary school, 22
  formative years, 19–23, 25
  high school, 29
  middle school, 29
  NBA All-Rookie Team, 46
  NBA All-Star Team, 47, 49, 68
  NBA draft (1989), 37
  NBA injuries, 52–54
  NBA playoffs, 9–10, 12–14, 16–17, 19–20, 49, 53, 62, 64, 68–70, 72, 75, 77–78, 82–83, 85, 87, 90
  NBA rookie season, 41–43, 46
  traded to Miami, 57, 61
  turning pro, 37, 39, 41–45

Western Athletic
  Conference Player of
  the Year, 32
winning Jack
  McMahon Award, 46

I
Indiana Pacers, 41, 45, 77

J
Johnson, Avery, 51
Johnson, Larry, 12–13, 83, 85
Johnson, Magic, 42, 47, 78
Jones, Eddie, 92, 93
Jordan, Michael, 19–20,
  44–45, 62, 78, 82

K
King, Martin Luther Jr., 22
Kohn Elementary School, 22
Kohn Middle School, 29

L
Lenard, Voshon, 64
Los Angeles Clippers, 53
Los Angeles Lakers, 42, 59,
  62, 78

M
Madison Square Garden, 70
Majerle, Dan, 16–17, 64, 83
Malone, Jeff, 61
Manning, Danny, 52–53
Marciulionis, Sarunas, 49
Mashburn, Jamal, 44, 66
Mason, Anthony, 92, 93
Miami Arena, 69
Miami Heat, 7–10, 10, 12–14,
  16–17, 19–20, 41–44,
  57, 61–62, 64–55,
  68–70, 72, 75, 77, 80,
  82–83, 85, 87
Miller, Reggie, 45, 77
Mills, Chris, 83, 85

Milwaukee Bucks, 39, 83
Mourning, Alonzo, 13, 62,
  64, 69, 72, 80, 83,
  85, 92
Muurseep, Martin, 66

N
Naismith Memorial
  Basketball Hall of
  Fame, 31
National Basketball
  Association, 7–8, 23,
  25, 32, 34, 39, 41, 43,
  47, 57, 62, 68, 75, 90.
NCAA, 31
Nelson, Don, 39, 41, 56
New York Knicks, 7–10,
  12–14, 16–17, 19, 45,
  62, 64, 68–70, 72, 75,
  77, 80, 82–83, 85, 87

O
Oakley, Charles, 16
Orlando Magic, 16, 51, 68
Owens, Billy, 49, 51

P
Payton, Gary, 46
Phoenix Suns, 43, 53, 61, 82
Pitman, Donald, 22–23, 25
Porter, Terry, 87
Price, Mark, 53

R
Rencher, Terence, 61
Richmond, Mitch, 37, 41
Riley, Pat, 7–8, 42, 57, 59, 61,
  64–66, 68, 77–78,
  80, 90
Robinson, David, 46
Run TMC, 41
Russell, Cazzie, 20

103

S

Sacramento Kings, 45
San Antonio Spurs, 46
San Simeon High School, 29
Seattle SuperSonics, 46, 49
Smith, Tony, 61
Sprewell, Latrell, 51, 56
Starks, John, 12–13, 44, 69–70
Stern, David, 47

T

Thomas, Kurt, 66
Toronto Raptors, 33

U

University of Michigan, 51
University of Texas-El Paso, 30–35, 37
University of Utah, 33
U.S. Army, 29
Utah Jazz, 44

W

Ward, Charlie, 12, 16, 70, 72
Washington Wizards, 41, 55, 68
Webber, Chris, 45, 51, 54, 56
Western Athletic Conference, 31–32
Williams, Buck, 13–14
Williams, Walt, 61
Willis, Kevin, 57

DATE DUE

3-2004	
MAY 1 8	